MW01047978

The Adventures Of Snibbles Mcgibbons

The Adventures Of Snibbles Mcgibbons

THE BIG MOVE

T.K. Connolly

gatekeeper press
Columbus, Ohio

This book is a work of fiction. The names, characters and events in this book are the products of the author's imagination or are used fictitiously. Any similarity to real persons living or dead is coincidental and not intended by the author.

The Adventures of Snibbles McGibbons: The Big Move
Published by Gatekeeper Press
3971 Hoover Rd. Suite 77
Columbus, OH 43123-2839
www.GatekeeperPress.com

Copyright © 2017 by T.K. Connolly

All rights reserved. Neither this book, nor any parts within it may be sold or reproduced in any form or by any electronic or mechanical means, including information storage and retrieval systems without permission in writing from the author.

ISBN: 9781619847064
ISBN: 9781619847071
eISBN: 9781619847088

Printed in the United States of America

Dedication

To my wife Brigid (Connolly) and
my kids Kate, T.J., and Timmy.

Thanks for all your inspiration!

This is the story of Snibbles McGibbons and all his Adventures. Snibbles is a young boy who has one older brother, Tibbles, who is seven, and an older sister, Kibbles, who is 9. Snibbles and Tibbles are a little different from most boys and girls – they both have red hair and freckles! But Mr. and Mrs. McGibbons told them not to worry. Everyone is a little different from each other. It is okay to be different from everyone else, because that makes you very special. Being a little different from others is perfectly okay.

This summer is very busy for Snibbles and his family. They are moving to a brand-new house in a new neighborhood! Snibbles is excited to visit the new house. The new neighborhood has a lot of dirt hills he can play on. He loves tractors and trucks, which are all over the place! Tibbles and Kibbles are also excited to move. They can't wait to go to their new schools and meet new friends. The new subdivision is just built and many boys and girls will meet new friends for the first time as well.

The day of the move was finally here! Mr. and Mrs. McGibbons were busy packing and cleaning up the old house. It was very exciting for Snibbles, especially when a huge gigantic moving truck showed up on his driveway! The biggest truck he has ever seen. A bunch of men jumped out to help with the big move. They very neatly packed all of his family's things into the monstrous truck, but then all of a sudden, they left. Snibbles was very worried things would be forgotten or lost and asked where the truck went. His mom and dad chuckled and explained it was heading to the new house – there was nothing to be worried about! All their stuff was on the way to the big new house and his parents promised nothing would be left behind.

Once he arrived at his new house, Snibbles was very happy. He strolled right through the front door. This felt like the biggest house he had ever seen! It was like walking into his own little castle made just for him and his family.

But it was so busy! Many people helped move all their stuff. His cousins were there – Dibbles, Nibbles and Zibbles. They wanted to help move stuff but mostly they were there to play with Snibbles while all the grown-ups filled the new house with their stuff. Snibbles couldn't be more excited and it was one of the happiest days he could remember.

Although they were thrilled to be in the new house, it was a very, very long day for Snibbles and his family! He was so tired. He knew it was getting to be bed time so he slipped into his favorite pajamas – the ones with tractors and trucks on them. He had seen so many new things this big moving day and couldn't wait for the morning for the discovery to continue. Then his mom tucked him into bed and read his favorite story. The last thing he remembered was his Mom whispering, "Sleep tight! Tomorrow we will meet our new neighbors and all the boys and girls on our new block."

The next morning Snibbles woke up early. He heard his mom cooking breakfast in the kitchen for Tibbles and Kibbles so he ran as fast as he could to join them. Everyone was so happy to be there in the new kitchen. The weather was perfect outside.

After they ate, the three McGibbons kids went into the back yard to play and to meet new friends. Mom was also meeting the neighbors. Across the subdivision, Snibbles could hear trucks and tractors building other new homes for more families just like his!

Snibbles played outside on the dirt hills with his siblings and new friends all day long and soon another long day was coming to an end. As Snibbles was on the way to bed, he looked up at his mother and said "Thanks, Mom! This place is great. I'm going to love it here."

The Adventures of Snibbles McGibbons

Snibbles Makes The Big Move

```
                      Q
                   F  E  S
                G  P  C  X  E
             R  O  A  I  O  C  L
          L  G  S  V  S  X  C  I  B
       Q  Q  T  T  E  N  W  F  V  T  B
    H  U  L  Q  X  U  T  G  R  I  G  I  I
    B  R  E  E  O  O  Z  J  T  R  U  C  K  N  N
 F  D  Q  J  B  O  D  I  R  T  H  I  L  L  S  G  S
V  R  R  F  R  I  Z  U  T  I  B  B  L  E  S  A  H  M  G
I  J  T  Q  A  U  K  M  E  G  L  F  N  E  W  H  O  U  S  E  C
    C  M  S        V  J  A        N  O  L
    U  I  O        I  O  X        Z  R  Z
    J  L  I        C  J  M        H  T  V
    W  Y  L        O  U  S        G  T  Z
    K  I  B  B  L  E  S  M  C  C  Q  T  U  Y  F
    L  U  S  H  O  P  A  N  C  Q  H  C  O  F  K
    Z  N  D  U  Y  U  M  D  O  V  P  O  S  K  M
    J  P  N  O  K  Y        B  O  A  O  W  R
    N  E  E  L  B  O        F  B  E  K  L  L
    I  U  I  G  H  W        I  M  I  J  O  Z
    D  E  R  M  O  V        N  U  F  G  U  D
    D  H  F  Y  S  W        Y  K  U  Y  C  V
    C  B  K  U  H  D        P  I  A  Q  F  M
```

WORD LIST:

BOXES	FAMILY	MCGIBBONS	SNIBBLES
CASTLE	FRIENDS	MOVE	TIBBLES
DIRT HILLS	FUN	NEW HOUSE	TRUCK
EXCITING	KIBBLES	SCHOOL	

pdfcrowd.com

The Adventures of Snibbles McGibbons

Snibbles Goes to School

```
            Y F J X T A T K
        H P Y W X Q C B I N D C
      E N A L I S N I B B L E S Z
      I D P M   E B B O     T K C Z
    R A F F K     Y H A S     E F D Y Z
    E E P A Q     P T V D     A G K E T
  R Y A C B R     M Y T N     C N F E Z C
  A A C I E N     U L N E     H P I Q I M
  P D Z L U S     B L V I     E Z D R E J
  M Q Q F Q G S D Z I C R F B R X S B Z B
  W K E B L X J B F B R F F A I L O Y Y K
  A U L V R F U M W I L L Y Y E O G Z T C
  L T U   J S B U Y N Z I Q E K E   Z B I
  A I O     S H D Y L L I N S D     I C F
  Y Y S     P O T O E W K N       E W D
  W S D E                     B Y L Q
    E S I N                 E T W J
      F R Z W T S C H O O L Z G K
      B Q Z Z G B V T P Q N R
        D Y C A U G F H
```

WORD LIST:

BILLY	DIZZY	READ	TEACHER
BOOKS	FRIENDS	RECESS	WILLY
BUMPY	FUN	SCHOOL	WIZZY
BUS	NILLY	SNIBBLES	

pdfcrowd.com

About the Author

As a real estate broker for more than 25 years, T.K. Connolly has moved dozens of families into new neighborhoods and has personally witnessed the excitement of countless children as they walk into their new homes. Tim has also seen firsthand the nervousness of kids going to new schools and meeting new friends. After a brain aneurysm and near-death experience, Tim decided it was time to put his stories to paper with *The Adventures of Snibbles McGibbons.*

Other books in
THE ADVENTURES OF SNIBBLES McGIBBONS
series.

Snibbles First Day of School

Snibbles Gets a dog

Snibbles goes on Vacation

Snibbles tries Sports

Snibbles goes to the zoo

Visit **www.snibblesmcgibbons.com**

CPSIA information can be obtained
at www.ICGtesting.com
Printed in the USA
LVOW06*2054130617
538000LV00004B/9/P

9 781619 847064